The Girl in the Title

by

Formatted by

Gimmicky Pseudonym

Author: Pseudonym, Gimmicky

ISBN: 978-0-6481463-4-6

Dedication:

CHAPTER ONE

ACKNOWLEDGEMENTS

I'd like to thank Gimmicky Pseudonym for creating this book to house my writing talent

OTHER BOOKS IN THE BLANK BOOK SERIES.

The Girl in the Title

Summer Beach

Silhouette of a Man

Not Lost in Space But Still in a Lot of Trouble

Journey to a Destination

My Life So Far

Fairy Tale

www.ingramcontent.com/pod-product-compliance
Lightning Source LLC
Chambersburg PA
CBHW071519100726
47908CB00004B/1225